OSSIA

향시

서지믄

SEO
JI
MIN

Published 2024 by the87press
The 87 Press LTD
87 Stonecot Hill
Sutton
Surrey
SM3 9HJ
www.the87press.co.uk

Copyright © Jimin Seo

First published in the USA by Changes Press in 2024

The moral right of Jimin Seo has been asserted in accordance with the Copyright, Designs and Patents Act 1988

ISBN: 978-1-0686446-2-7

Printed and bound by CPI Group (UK) Ltd, Croydon, CR0 4YY

Book Design by With Projects, Inc.

FOREWORD

Inside of translation are many constituent oppositions, many contextual proximities that line up nowhere else. It comprises and resists itself—in this book especially. The words lie down in angles around what is impossible to describe. And still, describing happens, or poetry does, revising, contradicting, sounding out a vaporous shape between two branching tongues.

OSSIA moves away from understanding, and dives instead into the lower wells of knowledge—the spaces we touch with abiding and potential feeling, which have been waiting for their lanterns. We need to confuse ourselves with many strategies to reach certain clarity, just as we need to detach from measurement to feel the full distance of the horizon. In this extraordinary, passionate debut, Jimin Seo takes up a material we think we recognize—language—and turns it, through permutation, historiography, and voyage, into a lyric, other terrain. OSSIA begins with a compressed narrative of a life, and unwinds the circumstances of that account to reveal finally an I, dual subject and object of regard, in all of the vast, radiant mystery of that position.

Seo does this by taking up both Korean and English and drawing them across the work into multiple modes of relation, none of them equivalence. Fragmentation, riff, homophony, analogy. A crown of sonnets sprawls like cuttings from a plant, yielding poems that grow in defiant new directions. Translation and retranslation triangulate to form the ghostly third that defines every relationship of two. Some of Seo's methods reveal themselves, but many do not, pulling the reader close to what is purposefully unknown.

The poems in OSSIA have a de-hierarchical posture that feels original and true. They communicate in ways that precede or survive the many conditioned expectations of how languages should behave. Octavio Paz writes that the first act of translation is the child asking his mother the meaning of a word. It is the human learning expression as a condition of humanness, and learning equally the impossibility of expression, the condition of having need and being in relation, drawing another inward with the incomplete means available.

This is a book calling to a mother—a teacher too, and lovers, and ultimately a self whose elements materialize through language even as the speaker laments what language cannot be or hold. OSSIA's poems flicker with sorrow and exaltation. They open and retrieve. They bear across and out.

Kyle Dacuyan

TABLE OF CONTENTS

PASTORAL

OSSIA

   14 Richard Asks Me for a Poem
   18 Richard Wakes Up in the Middle of the Night
   20 Richard and the Book Buyers

OSSIA

   28 Richard Asks to Sort Books Together
   30 Richard Remembers
   34 Richard Remembers Gide

OSSIA

   40 Richard Translates
   44 Richard's Metaphors
   46 Richard Tries to Set Me Up

OSSIA

   54 Richard Reads My Poems
   58 Richard Tells Me He's Old
   60 Richard and His Red Room

OSSIA

   64 Richard Has Trouble Sleeping
   66 Richard Asks Me to the Movies

OSSIA

   86 Richard's Exercise
   92 Ayre (himself remaining anonymous)

OSSIA

   96 Crown for Peasant Heads
   130 Translator's Preface

목차

24 깨어나라 깨어나라 옷먹어라
26 지기야 쌀 또 떨어졌어

48 불안한 제국

52 콩가루 집안

70 사랑하는 꿀벌 구름
72-74 지랄 떠는 그 새끼가 딸을파네
76 땅치고 후회하는 짓거리
78 얌다리 걸치는 남자
80 지저분한 결례같은 년
82-84 빨갱이 약속 편지

90 버림받은 자식

PASTORAL

You want me to tell you something about my life.
That I was carried to pay off a debt, two hundred
steps up an unremarkable hill my mother in 서울
defeated with the strength of a beggar's bowl, no
breastplate, a generous horse, a king-blessed épée.

A city you would recognize by ear in translation
or if I preach on the fickleness of the soul, how I
was knighted my name as a foal without a sex
by a father who chartered a flight in '81 to 미국,
beautiful land, married eyes blue and distant

as the Pacific. That I was blessed two good years
with my mother, conferred a boy by my hanging
anatomy, until she was called on to be a good wife
and chartered a flight into the afterlife or at least
what felt like its economy, distant from her own 몸

Reader, I've sold you my story. I am what you think
wrongly, half-beast, half-boy, too weak to carry
your pastoral flag, your mule-ride, cash strapped
belly-side. You ride and whip me into starlight. Rightly,
no time is enough time 잡아도 잡아도 지나가는 시간

OSSIA

Write about my body or another less Hellenistic one: Cadillac, Escalade, Rust: deer-field-sometime-car, fleshier if less sublime than the divine model every woman emanates in a man: Venus of Parts: doe-ish, dim. So let me snap off my hood, startle the cock making shit talk on my collarbone. Flash a knife, quarter this stag from its bushy thrust. Let me, sly under hide tender his three elegant legs, plug and mount them on my porny holes and run. Let me rear and knock koo-koo on any front door. *Tap-tap* quarter, a lap of water, kindnesses reserved for more congenial sex gods. Am I all messed up? A Venus of Migration, let me slant my neck to the half-lit chandelier and imagine my own family at the table. Take to the road humdrum radio thrum, chimeric limbs slant, hitch a ride, try my luck at the next town over. Tomorrow, find me gone from the lawn: head of fawn, torso, cherubic dawn.

13

시로 내 몸을 짓는 이틀아, 왜 또 나를 이 땅에서 지어 올리니? 오국의 여신으로 만드니 마음이 될 뿐뿐행하냐? 내가 걸을 들고 사슴을 죽이고, 짐승의 피를 언어, 잠을 다시 찾아가야 하냐? 검음 아래 언제나 피던 봉숭아 꽃 몸에 새겨진 남 엽집 향, 아무것도 모르는 풀밭 마음으로 태어나고 싶었지, 죽으면 그만이다, 너도 이 여미를 밭 름에 묶어버려라.

RICHARD ASKS ME FOR A POEM

Richard, an ill-considered nap is a horror in pink

but the head-burst between sleep and not-sleep

all dreams are faked and the vision self-televised

a phone call to the vault to get back for any price

what is the difference between a store-bought ghost

terror is knowing you will always be out of range and money

then the green out of doors a sure sign of spring the utter uselessness of it

the dream is over

tells me you are alive

as a wished-for buy

a body as I knew it

and an angel when real

a pink sky even

My friend, you haven't shown me a poem
in eight years! I'm not that angel. I'm still
alive and I haven't wings. If I really had
them, would I still take the *1* to school?
You've seen my gown with the open back
at the hospital when I've come wounded
by life. My point is the body can fail and
even my most prized assets are in danger
of fate's awkward strokes. A stroke is just
that, wing-smudged by a ridiculously better
dressed angel to remind us we are mortal.
At least, that's when an angel is true terror.
So use me while I'm useful. It's the reason
we met, your poems from your hands into mine.

엉뚱한 낮잠 자면 분홍색 입은 귀신이 나타난다
잠은 끝나고
잠들 자든 눈을 뜨든 봄꽃길이 머리가 터진다
살아있다고 누가 알려주고
모든 잠은 가짜다
TV 앞에만 살아 있다
돈으로 해결할 수 있다
전화로 돈 내고 예전처럼 돌아갈 수 있게
예전에 그 환경으로 돌아갈 수 있게
돈으로 산 귀신하고 천사가
무슨 차이가 있을까?
진실은 가치같이 한 푼 없는 삶이기에
분홍색으로 피어난 하늘
문밖에 새파란 봄 같이 쓸모없는 꿈이다

RICHARD WAKES UP IN THE MIDDLE OF THE NIGHT

My friend, no one tells you your mortal enemy
is yourself, waking up to the middle distance
between the marriage bed and the fridge, lamp
lit to a soft red glow so I can ford any river, pass
the brain fog and the forest of my subconscious,
slip two silvers to the bridge troll to walk back
into the palace of my lover sound asleep. Why
his pillow is the scent of my loss, and the quiet
rustle of bedding, dread, I sit softly at my desk
and hope light breaks sooner so I am less lonely.
Why do we wake up in the middle of the night
when no one wants it to happen? What friends
will take my calls when there is nobody home
to hear my incessant ringing. Who can pick up?

                    Richard, out of doors with drums and pipes,
                             nothing is as it seems. The car blare,
                                   musette, the night's music
                                         just beginning
                                            to crash
              into light. What's there to chase into myself but myself?

세계는 걸음 소리
휘파람 소리
눈에 들어오는 것은 믿을 것이 안 되고
빵빵대는 차 소리
무제트
밤에 나타날 수밖에 없는 음악
첫 빛을 꽉 박을 수밖에 없는 밤
뒤쫓아야 할 것은 내 자신뿐일까?

RICHARD AND THE BOOK BUYERS

My friend, I receive you in my voicemail.
That's the best I can do for now, I'm sorry.
Just as well to keep you on the ribbon tape
a while longer than your usual high tenor
wavers. Timorous. Ghostly. A bit of eternity
if an eternal shame another call will banish
your soul-voice to sell me on my paper's value.
No thanks. My friend's alphabet isn't fit for
purchase and I like their words near to me.
A poet's room *is* a grave, my dear—of friends.
Shout out their names and they shout down
hold me. Isn't love possession? In any event,
I'm happy to carry you in this device. I hope
I don't forget it. You're just swell. Bye dear.

                    Richard, forget it. Forget the lesion in my voice,
            forget-me-nots stuffed in the dismembered trough
        of my pig-idol throat, guardian to shopkeeper prayers
            every morning double their riches or at the very least
                not have their blood-child ruin what they built up
                  from nothing. I am a child of nothing that is to say
                  I am a child of books and the voice they sang
                    into my body, and like a ghost stole my voice
                      to sing whatever they have to say to you
                        in my first language, in every language
                      not for sale, not for sale, 사라지는 팔짜

지워라

그 목소리 속에 담은 상처를 지워버려라
묘에 울린 돼지머리처럼 풍만촛 꽃을 목 안에 쑤셔 넣고
술을 바미는 가게 주인의 돈이 거품처럼 부품는
불효자식들이 흙 안에서 울린 삶을 부셔버리는
나는 無의 아이다
나는 시 밖에 모르는 아이다
글이 내 음악이고
글로 내 밤을 지샜고
귀신처럼 혀가 입에서 날아가는
귀신처럼 혀가 돋아오는
처음처럼 끝까지 변함없이
못 파는 못 파는
vanishing destiny

OSSIA

What is this world to me
without that lodestar,
money? I am poor
and that's reason
enough to strip
the warm animal
that never belonged
on a junk Venus
to begin with.
This is it. Life
in this parallel
western where
wingèd things fall
off of me and I take
the mountain path
and kill my son
before it's too hungry
to eat. Still every
chorus is tragedy,
just like every girl
who falls in love
is my doing. What
ocean was ever
majesty? A Venus
is time travel.
Just another deer crossing
the multiverse.

날개를 달고 밤을 먹으러 나갔다. 두두둑두두둑 도망치는 짐승의 살. 따뜻한 어미 사슴의 배를 열었다. 자신 챙기지 못하는 사슴도 새끼 알리고 노력했다. 그 안에서 우주가 보였다. 구슬처럼 맑은 지식. 파란 밤에 떠돌린 피 먹은 달 심장. 꿈 모르는 결정의 바다. 짐이도 짐이도 불러주는 시간

Between two points of sleep they tell me I'm awake.
Alive is a kind of engine and I rev my dog

                                          and it walks me. Alive,

I'm inside of someone who hates me. My dog turns
on its body, takes a piss; and home, gnaws a bone

and sleeps. What is left there

                                  to dream of? Say

the bone hand of a knife peaks
and the steel pivots

through a soft hill of lungs and what could I possibly say
from that vantage of pain married silence?

Speak a field of black dahlias into red and think anything
I say saves anyone, myself

                          included?

Lion against knife against flower against this dog country
and somehow

                    what survives?

Dog that stirs like a greater beast. Set your sights on me.
Awaken, awaken, eat.

깨어나라 깨어나라 영원히라

The world starts with less than a penny

자기야 쌀 또 떨어졌어

Richard, to do nothing at last is to say the world
is at war again. The world is at war again and
the guns point west to east and east to west
and northwest of love war points inward
and each family scatters like dust brushed
off an old friend, my old friend, my love burst
from dust and the book I've found is never as I left it
remember it the spine broken from love and the hand that strokes it

RICHARD ASKS TO SORT BOOKS TOGETHER

My friend, I've made up my mind to climb up
the ladder myself. The Brits are hiding behind
the French, and the Germans in a ditch below.
An entire shelf for Proust and his acolytes and
Rilke can tip his prophetic hat to the Italians.
The Russians and Americans on the same case.
Save them the trouble of crossing the Pacific
to steal from each other. The Aramaic, Arabic,
and Hebrew god only knows what I'll do with.
Put them out next to Freud, Jung, and Melanie
Klein. What will I do about the Chinese? God,
when did I become a diplomat? The art books
you say? Put them on the very bottom shelf.
Art *does something* at last. A counter weight.

순수한 손들고 전쟁 밭을 걸었다
그 피 먹은 빨간 우주
어디를 봐도 총눈만 맞출 수밖에 없고
가족의 사랑은 타져 나간 먼지가 되었다
친구야 책 안에서 찾을 수 밖에 없는 사람 먼지 같은 친구야
기억 속에만 남을 수밖에 없는 부러진 들빼 같은 친구야

RICHARD REMEMBERS

>　　　　　　　　　　　　　　Richard, there is never enough
　　　　　　　　　　　　　to fill the middle ground between illness
　　　　　　　　　　　　plums fruiting in the street vendor's cart arranged
　　　　　　　　　　　the motive is which one is purple enough to kiss
　　　　　　　　　　to enter your flesh a second time to ask what is
　　　　　　　　What Moreau ever does right and never betrays his friends without

music in the background
and speech and body and
like a 3-part fugue and
and the answer, ready, ready at all
after satisfaction except hunger after all?
a simple kiss on the cheek?

My friend, you've rolled out the gold carpet.
What else are hospitals good for if not to tell
your friends time is not my friend? Tell me
to waste more of it on you. Bring me a pair
of socks I'll darn for fun, a satchel of plums
from that street vendor, the largest umbrella
I can fan out to block the ghastly white light
in Eden, Texas. Do I explain my doddering,
pocked as my brain is by the friction of casting
after my own name? I catch what light slips
me: the name of a fruit as color, the good
taste of purple, a visitor's too friendly voice
as if I too am divided into fractions. I won't
remember your name either, my dear friend.
You read me poems: mine and yours warped
into a pain I feel gladly—to remember.
We were translating *L'education sentimentale*
and I called it *A School for Feelings*. Bach's
4th French sarabande turned its repeat and
Moreau just betrayed Cécile with a kiss.
A body's betrayal is better with affection
I am at last feeling. School is out. See you.

등 뒤에 구름처럼 아무 의미 없는 음악을 떠올리고
불행한 말들을 썩은 목숨에 채워 넣었다
음악은 구멍가게의 자두처럼 피어나며
질문은 어떤 자두가 입맛에 맞고
입에 매달린 답은 입안에 채운 살이 되고
남는 것은 성성한 배일 뿐인가
입맞춤과 배설을 모르는 친구가 어디에 있을까

RICHARD REMEMBERS GIDE

Richard, I carry your immortal head on a platter and I am
immoral. Grief gives me pockets and I jam a wish through
none of which comes true. You ask for drips of ichor and
I wet your lips in shit instead the earth I know is what
you don't know and profane what mortals do best.
Up the stairs your head spits and I kiss your face.
You sing on the counter behind a closed door
les sons et les parfums tournent dans l'air du soir.

노래가 이거 아니면 뭘까

My friend, I say one thing to do another.
The dog must go out and forsake his leash.
The ball fit his mouth like a new shoe
bothers my feet but I let him run the palace
of my brain. Gide curls into Mildred's
stuffed arms, her glassy blues notched deep
into sight-slots as if a doll more than sees
the loneliness of an aging dog with a famous
author's name. What makes for marriage (no
not our kind) when Gide breathes his last
words into a fake? But did I know any better,
lining my lexicon as soldiers of the *république*
when anything private fails? My mistake
was breathing into a real body. A minor voice
in a manor I am at best a wary guest. May I
never be recovered into marriage. This kind.

                                                            What is song but that.

반산의 대갈봉을 쟁반에 듣고 오는 부드덕한 나

슬픔이 만든 주머니에 소말을 쑤셔 넣어도

내가 원하는 것은 비망이다

당신의 신의 피를 달라고 해도

피 대신 입에다 똘똘 발라주고

내가 앉고

당신이 모르는 것은 땅이다

야! 악마 같은 내 자신!

당신이 내 얼굴에 침을 뱉는다면

얼굴을 맞춰주겠다

잠거진 문 뒤에서 노래 부르는 당신

sounds and perfumes swirl in the night air

OSSIA

See the road and the deer that comes with it. Struck and arranged like pulp-Mary in Bacon's iconography, blood-pitched and tawny, red spade of tongue held and let go from a black rim mouth. Why say at all about sight when always, above the road is a pool of water, saltlick, and the horny fragrance of flowers. I know our body. I take your red into my red, push my breath against yours, and nothing of your great belly heaves old life. This border between us was never easy, I know that is no surprise. To speak is ecstasy. To kiss something else entirely. Your wine dries dark, my sound drowns in it. Did we kiss, sister? Why is it only when one of us is thrown to the road our cosmos is totally naked? A lake of red glass, where ripples of a bloody carp reveals life for what it really is—an accident where the profit body is transformed into a singular deer. What use is language when the ancients divide us into our final haunted constellations? Look up and see a mirror of what's already here! How comical to read stars into accident and present into future and mean it!

그래, 여기까지 해주마. 무당의 머리 위에 관처럼 내 혼을 얹혀주고, 너를 다시 만나주마. 어느 날 터진 사슴이 보일 거다. 사슴의 입에서 빨간 호수가 모일 거울처럼 내 얼굴이 비칠 거다. 살려 주진 못했고, 받아 먹을 살도 없고, 길가에서 썩어버릴 수밖에 없다. 미래는 짧다. 가을 속에 얼굴을 푹 틀잡고 두 눈을 깨물어라. 세계가 보는 너와, 내가 보는 너와 차이 없다.

RICHARD TRANSLATES

Richard, I have lost my language more times than I
can count. A deer comes herding past my bedtime
and tears the least fragrant buds from my garden.
If only all terrible things happen in our sleep when
nearest to death or birth before the canal of dreams
winks and the biology of wakefulness tells me revive!
revive! and I walk into the manicured lawn and all heads
are lopped clean and carried off in the acid sack of a thief,
the remainder the vibrant lush of slender leaves and sorrow,
what is the name of the giant you've become in the language I gave up,
the remnant sap rimming my mouth I shout

어두워진 사슴! 잊어버린 심장!

My friend, another giant of the world sleeps
for good. I'm asked to tug his tongue loose
a second time to revive him in a language
his own mother thought, *hardly vital*. As if
I could match that colossal trial between
maman and *la petite bête*. Latch him to a new
country. Wet my fingers in his mouth.
Drag his spittle up my throat, the unhinged
mandible, the soft plush of my own lukewarm
innards knowing my penning cuts him even
after his death. So why is it like leaving
a room after a disappointing night of sex,
my native tongue a sore point revised
as the last country he can never find relief.
Isn't learning a new language just a new way
of saying the world we live in isn't enough?
So why pry this giant's mouth open and
force my spit into his? Will his final rasp
burst in the air so I can convince the world
I was never good enough to bet his life on?

                                        deer of the night! Garbage heart!

예전처럼 돌아오지 못하는 허
밤 속에서 말은 할 줄 알아먹는 사슴처럼
왜 재수 없는 일들은 집에서 못 지내고
죽든 살든 눈을 뜨기 전에
이 몸뚱이가 깨어나랴! 꿈에서
깨어나랴! 하며 다듬어진 마닥을 찾으며
짤라진 머리는 도둑맞고
남은 것은 새파란 몸 같은 실망밖에 안되고
배신맞이 해가 얽던 도깨비 같은 이름은 뭐였을까
진몸을 입에 바르며

RICHARD'S METAPHORS

My friend, I'd very much like to see you
before your body winters down for god
knows how long this time. Of course, *I*
know the metaphors. Am I Peter or
the Wolf? A fool with a toy gun, cork-
for-brains, or do we call that bravery
only a child possesses, hunting his power
through a death trial he needn't adjudicate.
The Wolf is just hungry and winter makes
scant to warm his ribs fat, and what fills
him isn't Peter's flavor but a trial that says
death can be overcome by eating what
the season gives up. So have dinner with me.
The two-top at the *marquet* before I winter
down for good. The wolf dies you say?

                        Richard, I've eaten just enough to hate myself
               at the table of my enemy getting his fill to live.
          He sips wine after each bite of a rare cut of cow
            he nor I could point to in a butchery. He moves
                   to dessert and the cream rims his mouth
                      like a ringed planet, a glass of *digestif*
                        disturbing an atmosphere I have
                          no desire to expand. We were
                         lovers in the way Peter never
                          entered the Wolf. Sex, or
                        at least an approximation.

상 처럼 놓고 배 속 채우는 못마땅한 나
끌뵈기 싫은 밥 삼키는 원수
한 모금 한 모금 술 삼키고
어떤 살을 씻는지도 모르고
후시 한듯 입술 토성처럼 만드는 그 남자
환경이 짬아지는 소망
살을 모르는 연인으로만 남은
간식을 나눠먹는 남자

RICHARD TRIES TO SET ME UP

My friend, it would have been a match had he
not fucked it up. I know family is a sore topic
but if blood ties can be so neatly cut, it's good
practice to singe the loose ends with a lighter
so the rest of you remains more or less intact.
A scab isn't a bad deal, and even an old stump
has a good shot at renewal. Dear, if I'm being
perfectly honest, I'm scared. The last time you
were cut for being queer, you sat through eight
hours of exorcisms, a year after that flew back,
circumcised. What returns do we ever get for
suffering who we are? Shouldn't an occasion
for any kind of love be cause for joy? So don't
blame me for trying until you find one yourself.

                         Richard, distance is a coroner crowned
                              a slow sweet rot my head
                                 dropped on the counter
                        painted to mime an apple dearest
                                    inedible intensest
                                        red I kiss
                                  apple against apple
                    and your ghost bursts into sweetness
                    I can taste without ever having eaten.
                How like us. A mouth carved into the roundest
stone, eternal immutable fake, stone brushing stone after stone.

거리는 판 쓴 장의사
느리고 달콤하게 썩어가는
식탁 위에 올려진
내 대걀통 색칠된 사과
너무나 소중해 먹을 수 없는
그 빨강

사과를 사과한테 사람처럼 비비면
몸 안에 숨겨진 귀신이
달콤한 향으로 타진다 우리처럼
동그란 입술 색인 돌처럼
영원히 변하지 않는 가짜
스치고 스치고 굴러가는 머리

When making good is making good money.
A pocket sack empty
      save charity. *Brother,*
can you spare a dime? And I give
enough to feel goodness
      shrivel like the last
cadence of a 4-part hymnal: *A church won't*

take
a yellow fag like you in but what present is

history without one? That feelings are private
is no longer true. I sing
      with or without

one. Goodness at the lip of a bar, all I touch
yellows.

Whither bar you go and drink, tip the white 'tender,
and hung, yellow tender, wither. Perhaps

I should write about a different body,
a more white one. Perhaps
      Jimmy enters a bar
and shoots his shot. Perhaps
      every man drops
their fig leaf and Jimmy jukes out
like a Cellini. How like a classical beauty

to lose his nose, his modest cock flake,
and history at a gay bar is a coin in the realm

      of a fragile empire.

불안한 제국

OSSIA

I have a son and he is a poet. The poet eats from the head of my son and cuts a room into the air.
                        To be a poet is to have no dreams the poet says and hugs my son into his chest and tells me *we are lovers*, seals the air
                                    between us,
my son in any other room but my own.

My son, I bless you as a god is hired to do. I bless the knife that skins the fawn from its mother's field. I bless the fat between the hide, the flesh, ignites. I bless your dream, its bullet caught in the poet's bite.
                                Every day, may you triumph as you whip my hide in your hands, hope it's enough to buy another word,
                                  enough work for kingdoms to end my wars and like it.

도야지, 도야지, 내 몸 안에 구슬처럼 둥근 귀한 사람 열여라. 언제 팔, 다리, 입술, 눈동자, 달이 걸린 하늘이 다 너한테로 별처럼 떨어졌지? 아늑한 내 방 안에서 살을 맞고 자라긴 틀렸고. 언제 내가 나를 안고 둥을 쓰다듬어줄까? 왜 엄마 되는 물들은 자식 내어보내야만 할까? 갈라버리고 길에 던졌지, 달 하나 쏙 죽어버렸지.

And taking my body out of the house,
I empty into the street as gutter rain.
Store my mother in a reasonably sized
apartment and darken my dark room,
empty into a man and lock the rain
in his body and ask him if he can stay.

A boat in the river of my blood drifts
into a graveyard and there is little
I have to give in the way of offerings.
A bottle of soju, two legs of dried squid,
landlord-mums plucked to hide my rain.

Liquor-rain on my father's hair, I yank
the fish cud in half with my teeth, split
the fare between the grave and the crows,
barking. I have married a man to become
a more troubled poet, a more honest man,

a house less than a dusting of curd.

콩가루 집안

RICHARD READS MY POEM

                Richard, what is a lover but a reenactment

                to a corner the rain of apples dissembling

                our radiant queers holding hands as if what

                the round wound shelled into our backs as far

                in the kingdom of loneliness hopscotching after

                footbound shocked flamingo into flight by a cuss

                of a pink wingspan shrinking into the distant pink of himself.

the public holds

a pleasure to hunt

we resemble nears

back as we last

a lover tossed

shot, the absent flair

My friend, there is no such thing as a corrective
for an unfinished poem. Can you imagine telling
your lover to hurry up and get with the program,
when showtime is 100 days away with 90 percent
chance of thunder and rain? What I mean to say,
is that a lover should be undressed at his wettest,
his shirt and pants flung aside, his exposed beauty
beautiful for its fragility and willingness to always
be examined by every faculty and desire you have.
There can be nothing of your lover's body you can't
forgive: the wilderness of his damp hair, his weather
shy cock, a dark fruit you graze until he reappears
in your own body disguised as a heavy bruise you
carry with you always, anywhere and everywhere.

연인은 세상이 다시 그린
감옥뿐이 아닐까
비처럼 쏟아지는 사과를 피해며
기쁨은 눈물처럼 강처럼 흘러간다
몸 안으로 도망치는 빛나는 손을 꼭 붙잡은 귀어 인간들
우리는 등에 촛불이 밝힌 벌레가 되고
알 수 있는 건 혼자 있는 외로운 왕국뿐이다
연인을 찾으러 돌 치기 놀이처럼
발을 하나 묶고 돌을 던지는 곳마다
놀란 물망이고가 남아 도망친다
그 남아간 반자리는
먼 거리에서 분홍색 날개가 작아지면서
연인 내면으로 사라진다

Richard, I've broken every promise I've ever made
to a man I undress fireside the day's stink discarded
into the fire the smoke rising like some ill-gotten fortune
an elephant under the canopy of a bodhi tree crying
for the secret oasis of his herd or anyone who looks like him
until the rain wipes out the vision and all that's left is a lie
the present man and the past undressing to music he can't lie to.

RICHARD TELLS ME HE'S OLD

My friend, there's a secret palace I take off
my clothes in to fix all claims my lovers
have tucked away from me. A marvelous
dressmaker's doll as Adonic as I remember
my twenties, attractive enough to gloss
my inner forgeries as if that matter kept me
from haunting sex with companionships
steered off-kilter when it was good enough
to last. Now my secrets are on purchase.
Adonis dressed in my golden past as I buy
stock in each of my well-endowed wounds.
I have lost more of my hair, and my body
brags longevity by my cock's mere pissing.
I'm old enough to turn my head and look back.

후회 없이 깨져버린 약속
그 남자를 난 물 앞에 세워놓고 옷을 벗긴다
하루의 격양된 약취를 물 속에 태워버리고
올라오는 연기는 재수 없는 팔자처럼
보인다 보살 나무 아래에서 눈물을 흘리는
비밀 같은 식구를 찾는 코끼리를 색칠한다
비가 그 팔자를 지워버린다
남는 건 거짓말 같은
얼만 보는 남자와
지나간 남자
진실밖에 모르는 음악 속에서 발가벗은 나

RICHARD IN HIS RED ROOM

My friend, you want to know how it feels?
Why so much red in my life as if to mirror
blood running in my body? What counts for
an interior paramour when *my* spirit versus
my flesh becomes sport? Who keeps score
when I buy red camellias and steal a holly
from my landlord's planter? My dear, if I'm
put on thinners, and a clatter of pills governs
my body's betrayal, shouldn't I room in red
exuberance of what my richest red allowed
before I became this hollow? Who knows
what will go first? Age makes carrion and
mind shrinks to a peephole. And the spirit,
a precise science, burns in the nether ether.

             Richard, where do I go with these feelings my blood
                    wrung from point-finger to shoe and the patient
                  body says you are not dying I say I am more than
         sure refusal is refuse what passes for suture pooling my dread-
                 spit into flight my wings catch nothing but future and humor,
                bile, piss, snot, companion to the sure rotation of my mind
              around body when all I want it to do is stop the traffic says go
       and the digital icon walks me step by step cross into a blazing red sky.

꿈은 피를 어디로 가져갈까
손가락에서 신발로 떨어지는 피를 어디로 가지고 갈까
참선한 몸이 죽지 않는다고 해도
마음이 거절당하는 돈은 쓰레기나 다름없고
체매진 상처는 공포에 섞인 날개 달린 짐이고
잡을 수 있는 작은 미래뿐
쏠개즙 지린 오줌 곳물
몸 위에서 뺑뺑 도는 머리가
고통을 무시하고 새빨간 하늘을 찾아가라고 한다

OSSIA

At what point did I collude collision and dream? That a deer on the road is dearest sister. That I am more warm animal for killing her to civilize my own great fires. I thought anyone driving furiously towards you was not a lover but a photograph and a crime scene of how the world really works. In acts of great love we do nothing.

꿈이 힘이 닿았든 세계에 펼쳤었다. 세상은 둥글 듯했다. 세계는 둥그리미이다.

Richard, I am awake and the heater hums into my feet because
it's Spring and I am not ready for renewal. The stove is lit
and I count each burst of blue flame when a great fire
is never counted on one or a hundred fingers.
It is by duration, how long can I last
singly in a bed, or in two,
measuring the distance
of Gabriel's breath
until I stop mine
and extinguish.

RICHARD HAS TROUBLE SLEEPING

My friend, I'm having trouble sleeping.
I've tried to run the sheep count to zero
but can't help but wonder where it is
they fall off to, if I'm killing off one
hundred dreams to save just one of mine.
Pastorals don't work when you save
the pasture's green to toss the rest
to the pit. But then again isn't the brain
an orderly farm and livestock fodder
to feed the harmony of my body-house?
If a farmhand mends the fence and takes
a pig to slaughter and dinner is ready,
what will my body kill to mend the well
-spring of my mind? What is forgettable?

눈을 볼 수 없는 봄

발가락에 기어오르는 뜨거운 바람

살아나갈 준비가 안 된 눈동자

나도 불을 켜놓고

그 터지는 파란 불길 속에서 하늘을 찾는다

얼마나 혼자 지는

얼마나 둘이 되는

사랑하는 가브리엘

숨 거리 찾으며

내 숨은 입에서

시간처럼 흘러나간다

RICHARD ASKS ME TO THE MOVIES

My friend, do you want to see a movie?
Brighton Rock at 8 on the pier. A touch
on the nose, but what's a crime of love
with no audience and candy to sweeten
the plot? Is there anything more terrible
than a lover who tries to kill you to skip
out of town, unscathed? It isn't that, is it,
but the awful lengths we go to disguise
love's terror between a feathered gown
and a sharp black suit. Show too much
and too little of our hand. Who doesn't
want to choose themselves first, even
in perfect union? Just once, to eat the last
slice of sky not caring at all who's there.

                              Richard, I have everywhere to be good
                                  and happy I steal from the hole
                                      the business of change small
                                            set loose in the arena
                             of my tongue ants their work-fire
                                 sure-harm rests best in a hole
              the blister of a small life stained in the saliva I spit
                    swallow, the insect-body my muscle plucked
            from the hole everything is mine and borrowed the heart
the protean junk the pincer the mind and the terrible holy spirit.

손이 가는데 마다 불꽃이 터진다
구멍가게에서 훔친 동전은
몇 푼 되지 않는다
흙집에서 파낸 개미를 옷바닥에 풀어놓으며
상처는 구멍에 내버두는게 좋지 않을까?
죽기 싫어하는 개미가 쳐들 듣어먹
난 그 상처를 삼키고 쓴맛을 안다
집에서 뽑아낸 개미의 근육과
심장
집게발이
내 구멍 속으로 들어오면서
땅에서 발린 모든 것이 내 쓰레기 같은 내 마음의 집이 된다

OSSIA

I am neither divine or the garden like it. No difference, what's taken away, and what I've given up. Why come here then, the angel's trumpets scant suggestion of music. A new karaoke that says *come hither* from a dusk-gold rapeseed disco. But what is promise if not slaughter and yield? An animal's call and response of here I am to take off my work and scatter my divinity to the winds, come to find something like home or nothing like it, lives? Would it be any other garden than a farm?

흔들었다. 음악을 따라갔다. 노래 불렀다. 아 이 아 이 내 이음으로 받들 더럽혔다. 입에서 똥 냄새가 풀러나왔다. 우 우 우 자식들이 울었다. 우 우 우 우 짐승들도 울었다.

Such a sorry sight the shirt cut on
my wife. The sorry husband cut out
of marriage, a wedge
of cut lime held   doggish,
and alive if that

       is the right word. I am sorry

death is terrific.   I wear my wife
to the market, sweep
her through the aisles
of olives and figs: tinny grove,
epoxy, music.

I wear my wife to bed   hurry
and strip   my shirt floored,
jagged,   a strip
of cut loin,   red traffic,
sweat.

I wear my wife   to my wedding
cut handsomer   by flowers.
I wear her as a new wife.   A rag
of her hair   cut and stowed
under my pillow.   I wear her,

coloratura queen,
         mockingbird,
            light,
          less light,
beloved parade   of bees.

사랑하는 꿀벌 구름

My language is a worry
the world can't convince
me I'm right.

I'm a man who hugs
head-cocked
into an abacus. I kiss

the dirt with my knees,
count the last bar
of my wife's song.

I lose my wife
to a bet. Hang
a sign she can't see

on her wrist. Tie
up her hair
in a pony,

yoke her to a
marketplace,
give up my riches.

지랄 때는 그 새끼가 딴놈팔네

My wife gives
children I wanted
and dies.

Pay off my debt,
debtor. Move her to a vault
where no fault

is this honest: endless
green beauty
with lightning streaks,

an odor of doubt
brocaded on my coat.
A bastard digs his own pothole.

He asked about the price of the land,
the square mile of river coast,
their taste for salt:
river kissing ocean as if
brine cradled between two
mortals signals the same mythic union.

His marriage watch, the vow
of rings, he asked to sell
with the great interest
of a new husband.
He asked if he would be happy
with his wife. If they would grow old
and die peacefully in their sleep.
The lender, attractive
in the way a salesman agrees to,
nods, and takes the sale.

In his 64th year, the land's increase
two-fold, he throws his wife
into the river and her ashes dust
his home's increase. He marries
twice, carries out the sale of the land,
the sale of his first wife, licks
brine from a puddle of tea, sips
to quiet the ocean of his first life.

딴치고 후회하는 짓거리

I brush the sheep to sleep.
Warmth coiled between
a tangle of uselessness
and business: a winter coat
I'll love, a paired glove
to mute his callused hand,
a wet shirt dry before
drunkenness comes
and the question
of his body's knife
suspends between
my throat and his kiss.
Is this the business
of every wife? To stay
my sheep's enormous
appetites? How like
the father my lamb comes,
less and less in the way
a marriage will fail
and still last. Sink
my lamb to sleep,
flick the oven wick,
carve a roast for two,
pinch my rosy dimes,
rosemary, thyme,
swallow a knife,
my man's legs slung
over two wives.

안다리 걸치는 남자

How much time do I have left
to wash
between my thighs, pity
the form

washed up in the bath, repent
the piss
stain merging into the greater
body

when the husband departing
his job
kisses his wife, kisses
his sons,

takes his chair to slice his meat,
choicest
cut on his plate, kisses
his own

red lips to a dead animal,
clean as
he can possibly be
to receive

a woman as filthy as a used rag.

지저분한 걸레같은 너

Here the red sun sinks. Aches
from pulling down the tent,
throwing back her unwanted good

into the truck. Aches for the money
she'll have to make up, perfuming
her pillow as she breaks a dream

she's too tired to take with her.
Whose life will she want to live
today? The clouds part

to the unrelenting present:
A shirt she doesn't mind
losing, a globe of red rice

for strength, drives back
into the same plot to work
her soft sons. Today,

there is a need for bicycles.
To hoist the aluminum
with her blood's heat, bolt

her history into the wheels
of a glittering saleable machine:

빨갱이 약속 편지

*Dear customer, in a city far
from here, a summer ride
meant collecting the rain*

*in my ears, and my eyes
find anything worth selling.
A thousand spins for nothing*

*more than hunger carried
like a sack of rain rich air,
or on a lucky day, finding*

*a red flyer to trade in
for a hundred paper 원
telling me how living*

*ought to be, in a promise
penned by a communist.*

RICHARD'S EXERCISE

반으로 쪼개진 몸이든
어떻게 진실이 머리통 구멍 안에서 살아남을 수 있을까?
추억은 사슴한테 뜯어먹힌 빨간 정원 밖에 안 되고
전쟁에 날려버린 장미꽃도 분신으로 변해 버리고
모든 역사를 잊어버리겠다
이 몸도 잊어버리겠다
해에 불을 붙이고 태워버리겠다
지워버릴 수밖에 없는 내 몸의 역사
처음에 열린 역사
내 마음의 분신
Busted planet! Burst of dust!

여기까지 와서 뭘 포기할 수 있을까
구멍에서 빠져나간 해도
이 몸 덩어리의 분신 돼 버리고
빨간 안방에서 시간 버리는 내가
텅 빈 머리통을 주먹으로 두들겨 패면서
빨간 유리 안의 바람도 훌어버리고
이렇게 축역을 살려달라고 부탁해도
진심이 진심 될 수 있을까?
뭐
목숨은 똑같은 목숨이겠지
반으로 쪼개진 둘이든

My friend, it's a pity I didn't think to invent
a new body until now. No chance my outer
petals attract a bee, much less a model kiss
my cheeks save in a friendly way. No, it's
whether I'll survive a fall, stumble with dignity,
lock arms with a friend everywhere we go
granted that sounds rather pleasant. Twice
a week, I ascend the demisphere and wave
my arms to find solitude as firm as a monk
who's given up his family, his job, his sex
in exchange for time to figure out if his body
was worth the price of his spirit and his mind.
Is it any wonder I did it in reverse? My mind
a wonderfully stocked library in a drafty tower.

that is how I remember your fiction as my fiction
as my life and yours
smelt together like a stone split into dust and spit
into fiction how do I
remember anything truer than the fiction of how
your body is a red garden
a herd of deer eats into and the war of the roses
is a fiction and a history
everyone I know and you know forgets into a fiction
that anything you will be
is lost unless the flame is counted by everyone we know
but will forget and move on
move on in the language of my birth the language of my truest fiction
빼개진 우성! 타진 먼지!!

Richard, I give up my fiction and the language you speak
gone from your body

is my body's fiction and the hours I visit your body
in your red room

is the empty room of your mind is a fiction I blow
my life into a red glass

The lake receives my child
is one way of saying
you are drowning.

An echo ripples across time
and dissipates into a lush
soundlessness. A soft

lap and a black brush
of hair on the shore
-line as if there

is ink enough to write,
lake, bless my child
as a new way of seeing:

A warm bath drawn for me
to sink my garbage
tongue, buoy

past the tubby lip, sink
into a towel,

어미
어미
wait for me

버림받은 자식

AYRE (HIMSELF REMAINING ANONYMOUS)

Child, my world-scape sways.
My final bedtime. My attendant
music. So short, what you take.

Will you leave when I'm done
leaving? Or soonest mended,
yourself go early? 10 o'clock,

I am dying. 10 o'clock who is
leaving. Whose planet spins.
Whose organ bedside, sings?

Pinned: whose constellation rot.
Whose starlight wrought. Child,
whose eternal ping this blackening

mine will mind? Nevermind
my throat its miscarriage, trot.
Nowhere my sirens internal

syrinx, stop. Pegasus. Corvus.
Sphinx. Delphic mouthpiece,
shrink. *10 o'clock, 10 o'clock.*

OSSIA

My enemy, how do I find you in this terrible museum of used goods: bills of sale, foot traffic. How many times do I enter this city of bodies greener and richer than me, holding a ticket to revisit my pasts? Nike, I return victory to you, this handsome head cast by a lucky stroke: a mortal American blond struck by a car, which I could kiss should I want it for myself. A husband remade isn't a bad idea if there is such a thing as a modular lover. Do you remember yours? He bet your life at the casino and that's how you got here, Nike of Samothrace. First stop at the Louvre. Beheaded. If I'm honest with myself, I'm lonely. But do I even want someone like you? A lover who flies away,
                a pyrrhic
                              victory?

친구를 떼어 놓고 여행이 길어졌다. 여행이 일상으로 변했고, 삶은 남편의 골목에 갇혀버렸다. 이제 여기까지 와서 누가 내 혼에 담긴 느구렁이를 건져줄 수 있을까? 고무신 같은 문은 벗었고, 때문은 얇막 같은 정을 떼어 버렸고, 글쎄 그래도 도돌 뜨고 건너왔나 보네, 우순아, 너도 여기에 왔니?

CROWN FOR PEASANT HEADS

Space rumbles in the catalogue of ills.
Speed, cause, spells to inevitably spook
cor into *corpse*, to only know a book
is curse, cur, or cure until
too many beers down incantations spill
at the men's bar the boys so remarkably still.

So let me on the dance floor the last fox look
chicken: galaxy disco: *coeur de poulet*: cuck.

Get down or boogie up the groove digs just
the same: how many tongues will I numb
into kiss: how many tomes will I thumb
out of hiding, a fox, a cock, a hard crust
of dirt broken to rummage the soft thing
living used to be—that incandescent thing.

떨리는 우주가 내 마음의 아픔

Living used to be that incandescent thing.
To make much of a rock before the toss

makes less: the hand that held, the soft
kingdom of grass in red. The dinner ring

I wait for doesn't come. What rings
is the wingbeat of a hawk taking off

a fox cub from its cud. Hawk who injures
under cover of hunger take me out of this

loss: bed with love of my life dead—yet
why is it fox still runs my heart hereafter?

If hereafter means hawk continues
to knock its beak first into an incense pot

is what fox blooms from his mouth asters
from a grave too? What does it mean to
                                        speak then?

언제 다시 내 삶이 빛날까

What does it mean to speak from a grave then.
Who makes a bed from out of season
asters, irises, questions of when

the corporation sends its condolences. Reason
there is no insurance that covers *thanks
for coming, this means so much*. To whom

do I direct the most sincere regards and rank
distance relative to blood, museum
paltry grievances and encrypt

your death as a semiotics of flowers.
Asters in a lap of Egypt.
Irises, power.

So how do I erase the dusk in your voice?
Ai ai ai you seemed to say with no choice.

무덤 앞에서 마음을 바람 속에 놓아보면 무슨 의미가 있을까

Ai ai ai you seemed to say with no choice.
On a different day, I lay with a man
and said *ah* not caring if the song was *man
on the moon* or *earth, wind, and fire*. Your voice
at the end of the call said there is no noise
where two men live only two men can
die. I wish I knew then what angel you meant,
flying on a crushed wing, circling, circling
as I lay with Gabriel and said *ah*.
Why is it two men to each other the sun
is certain doom to go? Clothes doff
like feathers, the light flickers *ah*
and how a voice you know is your son
grappling his better angel, *Ai Ai Ai*

얘 얘 길이 얘 얘 언니

Grappling his better angel, 아 아 아
she's dead. Will she astonish a real
marriage there as the men's *ha ha*

make house in fever reels   here:
sweat, dust, money just shy to feel
what it's like to be untended.

Will she find persimmons to peel,
cut, fatten herself unwedded
master of the house unbedded.

Why did the angels make good women
suffer marriage with piss poor men?
Why is it the myth of men to triumph

unfairly. Why is she written this way?
Where is she who triumphs anyway?

천사를 붙잡고 흔들어도 아! 아! 아!

Where is she who triumphs anyway
Is survival the last measure of it
The west is a desert and a highway
The east a sea to toss trinkets
a room I love because you are in it

The distance the body goes to hide
in it: sew names on a blanket
slide bouquets of asters inside
a bed to drift drowsily downward
a dream because you are in it

The unspeakable sum sickness incurs:
a debt of marriage, children, a well-lit
funereal face sweeps like a censer
and triumphs all rooms you enter

어려움 없이 길을 받던 그녀는 어디 갔지

And triumphs all rooms you enter
even if the work is badly done and
the motto is *good-for-nothing* and

even if a kiss is mist on a sore back and
something in me breaks into a center
-fold of soft money on glossier lovers

why not our bodies vanish and
re-vanish into lightning, voodoo, and
this last contract we choose to enter.

Do I eat at the dark as the wild fox eats
a Spartan girl through her back
and exits, bloody snout, into the woods?

What are the small games you hunt to live?
What animal eats me so you too may live?

밤마다 밤마다 불빛이 피어나네

What animal eats me so you too may live?
Dry peppers to pad his shoes—*his* wife—
light of his feet, ready what a good wife
is told to do: help him be his mount, live
under contract of a pen and make a sieve
of my throat and quietly bray *m y l i f e*.
And this is what my boy sees: a bad life
is a bad marriage is a bad wife. Please,

here is my arm, take it. The woman
who clothes you brings down a knife
and cuts off what feeds you: my arm
as a translation of fate is where a man
is the swan but only I must change my life.
Light my own feet on fire. Do some necessary harm.

네가 살수있게 어떤 짐승 속에 집을 만들었니

Light my own feet on fire? Do some necessary harm?
This is my history or is it just money: petrol,
candy, a standard oriental car. How charming
to let a man's pistol cock and watch patrol
rummage my body and arm a quiet blindness
in me and let damage slip out of time.

What is it I'll pay for now? Neighbor I miss
my car. Neighbor I burn the road in wine.
It's dinner time neighbor. Won't you stay please
stay. If I run out of my body and let the husk
divide like the segments of an orange, release
me from acid, sugar, this hunk's terminal musk

will I light your feet on fire? Brother of course
you are not there. Your life is a matter of course.

밤에 불을 피고 누구한테 피해를 선물할까

You are not there as a matter of course.
You carry the box you dust in. You kick
the dog wayside, no telling what's worse:
the damage you carry or damage picked
clean from the teeth and spat out. What
is hurt when your own animal yelps
and retreats to a corner of the room? What
bares better its knives and cleans a bone
than your own cruel fangs. You animal.
You master of damage. You bad dog.

What light comes through this minimal
heaven to rattle the dustbin you're dogged
in? All your weight slung into this white hole.
Where have you been this whole time? Where?

그래 내가 없는 것이 당연하지

Where have I been this whole time? Where
to be measured by what I do and not by what
I am.

    The People United Will Never Be Defeated,

yet even here the same mother bear
trots her cub, leery of a shot supersonic
to the soft canal that is her heart defeated.

Where does she deposit her ear, so little
left of the handsome fish she's taught
to chase, rip, and parcel out until its taut
unraveling foams her reddening spittle.

Your kind are dying she hears in a high whistle:
all day birdsong, fireworks lit-up from a cot.
Cross the woods and it's still run and be caught.

    United My People Will Never Be Defeated/a riddle.

그럼 내가 어디 있을까

OSSIA

Better to write history as I see it.
Better and better to eat dirt, eat shit
on a fall, plug my blood in grease,
spit; let pin my ribboned hurts on
a transcendent donkey as it works
out of its divine perturbations—poor
soul—my little more than blind ass,
pray, take what you can get and save it.

OSSIA

¡El pueblo unido, jamás será vencido!

United my people are never defeated. A riddle
after all, is a winsome set of numbers,
crumbs, a lottery of what ifs so meager
we pilfer our neighbors and still read *this is kibble*.

Who is it who eats without worry, quibbles
less over who gets more billing for sugar,
go dutch and wonder who affords
desire under immigration or fail nobly poor.

Is this the kind of meal we pay for? Always,
a wallet filled by the company we clothe,
make much ado about food, tender out, and fuck
until our bodies fill and a new fortune
cracks at the next table and equipoise
teeters with you, child, plucked
                              from a newish star.

가족이 된 백성들은 패배를 모르는 난제

Child plucked from a newish star I refuse
you address, your bread, your citizenry.
Play your friends your grim wizardry.
Abracadabra I'm dead.

                          Why believe refuge

is the trunk of one husband. Recuse
my will for bread. Why husbanded
and besotted bride be good husbandry

when it's my pony to ride. To refuse
marriage. A house. This country's
ticker tape parade in endless red confetti.

What do I make of you? A magic trick
where I'm sawed in twos, you, a dog
dead in a sack. Do I drop you down river, too?
Kill everything you eat. Understanding is ruin.

새 별에서 마을에서 나의 아이야

```
Kill everything you eat. Understanding is ruin.
     everything you eat.              ruin.
Kill                  Understanding   ruin.
               you eat                ruin.
Kill everything                       ruin.
Kill                  eat. Understanding
               you eat                ruin.
               you
     everything               is ruin.
               you                    ruin.
Kill                                  ruin.
               you            is
                     eat      is
                                      ruin.
```

입에 넣는 모든 것은 죽어다 이해는 파멸이다

TIN CROWN

Dear Child—My Trembling Universe—,

Did my life ever light, fire?
What wind dissolves kismet from a grave?
Ah! A road
or even an angel to pin down and shake, ah!
Where is she who breaks wild
room after room after room fireflies unfolding!

What animal do I house so you live?
To whom do I make a present of you, carnage?
Yes, of course you are not there.
Then, where is it I go?
A family united eats defeat—never. A riddle,

My Child—My New Star—,

Kill everything you put in your mouth. Understand ruin.

관

롤라는 우주가 내 마음의 아픔
어제 다시 내 산이 될까
무덤 앞에서 마음의 바람 속에 들어 오는데
아 아 아 안 갚 있네
천사를 붙잡고 흔들어도 아이 야
어제 없이 갔음 받아 그는 어디로 갔지
반마다 이야이 괴롭히 괴어나네
내가 살 수 있어 아예 점순 속에 장든 들었나?
불에 물을 떠고 누구한테 대해줄 선물일까?
그래 내가 있는 것이 당연하지
그럼 내가 아디에 잘들까?
가족이 된 빠성들 틀벌래 누군가 를름까?
새 벽에서 공해 나의 아이아
안에 눕는 모든 것은 죽어라 이해는 파움이나

TIN CROWN

Dear Child—My Trembling Universe—,

Did my life ever light, fire?
What wind dissolves kismet from a grave?
Ah! A road
or even an angel to pin down and shake, ah!
Where is she who breaks wild
room after room after room fireflies unfolding!

What animal do I house so you live?
To whom do I make a present of you, carnage?
Yes, of course you are not there.
Then, where is it I go?
A family united eats defeat—never. A riddle,

My Child—My New Star—,

Kill everything you put in your mouth. Understand ruin.

관

떨리는 우주가 내 마음의 이픔
언제 다시 내 삶이 빛날까
무덤 앞에서 마음을 바람 속에 풀어놓으면 무슨 의미가 있을까
아! 아! 아! 길이 없네
천사를 붙잡고 흔들어도 아! 아! 아!
아려줌 없이 걸음 밝던 그대는 어디로 갔지
방안에 방안에 불빛이 피어나네
내가 살 수 있게 어떤 작은 속에 집을 만들었니?
방에 불을 피고 누구한테 피해를 선물할까?
그래 내가 없는 것이 당연하지
그럼 내가 어디에 있을까?
가족이 된 백성들은 패배를 모르는 난제
새 별에서 떠온 나의 아이야
얼에 넣는 모든 것은 죽여라 이해는 파멸이다

TRANSLATOR'S PREFACE

It's backwards whatever we have to say. The bodies are most beautiful, dead. A stretch of sky so white-lit the spittle I unloosen wets: a watercolor:

the bodies were

for instance: my loves mimed into an opera of chairs filled and unfulfilled. My lovers bound in twirls of cellophane into a car, a shirt tossed to the bed, shirt that fills my body like a shadow. Speak I say and I spit into the hole of my loves, wet their interiors, loosed and loose into the night-hot sky the bodies were

only myself unbuttoning

하늘이 바다고
바다가 하늘이다
땅은 시들어가는 시간처럼
먼지를 업고 세계를 떠나버린다

memory / migrate
translate / memory
My loves rot like scrap
-loaded ants turning in

to a peephole: may I be understood like this: *There there* as a comfort I've never heard of but there, there a space point specifically to wander

여기저기 여기저기

SEO

JI
자
MIN
자

올림
let me raise our name

PRAISE FOR OSSIA

"*OSSIA* is thrillingly alive. There's an inventive daring at work in the lines that feels at times like a song, at times like the voice in your head, telling you about yourself and others, everything you do and don't want to know. One part intimate self-regard, one part provocation, this lyric extension of a conversation between friends, between mentor and mentee, the living and the dead, lover and beloved, pursues a series of renewals as the poet offers the poems in Korean and English, hoping to include all of the registers of his feelings. The result is a gorgeous game of language and poetry, conducted for the highest stakes: love."

Alexander Chee, author of *How to Write an Autobiographical Novel*

"To enter *OSSIA* is to step inside a haunted house, a hall of mirrors, and an echo chamber all at once. At the outset, Jimin Seo's speaker (disguised as himself, or himself in disguise) offers traces of a family history marked by abandonment and loss, and one whose legacy includes a habit of retreating into one's headspace so deeply that anything outside it, even one's own body, seems strange, and too unpredictable to approach—except, of course, through language. In other words, he is made a poet. 'I am a child of nothing,' Seo writes, 'that is to say / I am a child of books and the voice they sang / into my body.' Fortunately, Seo comes to share a life-defining friendship with the legendary poet Richard Howard, a bond so magical that the late Howard's voice is virtually resurrected in the book's ongoing dramatic exchange. Parts of this back-and-forth appear also in Seo's native Korean, which recurs throughout the book as if from the speaker's alternate (ossia means 'alternatively') linguistic perspective. Uncanny, gorgeous, wise, exhilarating, and driven to represent the messy business of subject formation as accurately, but as exquisitely, as possible, *OSSIA* is an extraordinary achievement, and unlike anything I've read before."

Timothy Donnelly, author of *Chariot*

"Abounding with ghost and animal voices, Jimin Seo's *OSSIA* makes a radiant and enchanting debut that musically oscillates between Korean and English. There is a mythological tone that permeates the collection, that tells and retells themes of death, birth, and rebirth mainly in the form of letters and incantatory address. One does not need Korean reading ability to fully relish in the linguistic prowess and hypnotic imagination of this collection. And yet, it is impressive how the bilingual presentations of poems invite stimulating questions of how and when images and figures are conjured and transformed amidst processes of revision/re-vision—adding to our meditation on the book's themes while positioning the act of translation as a rich, creative, and spiritual act of communication. I am eager to witness this book to cast its luscious spell on both Korean and English-speaking literary communities."

Emily Jungmin Yoon, author of *Find Me as the Creature I Am*

"In Jimin Seo's debut collection *OSSIA*, the lyric catches between the art of living and the living of art. Vibrant poems oscillate between languages and queer intimacies, that erotic and operatic space between there and—after a breath—there again. In a collection that is bilingual, bifurcated, hybrid, diasporic, *OSSIA* reminds me of hocketing. A song shared between two voices where one voice sounds to allow a partner some rest. What rest? 'A poet's room is a grave,' Seo writes. So the tender song in the background of that room crackles with the refrain of how to care for the living. Then the dead. Between two bodies, there, in that melodic fission and frisson, poetic life is thrillingly interrupted. 'I catch what light slips me.' Yes. That contrapuntal slippage. The fugue from the title. *OSSIA*. Alternate. To do by turns. And, in turn, to worry wondrous language. In order to sing virtuosic translation."

Jay Gao, *Imperium*